FISH
SOUP

FISH SOUP

URSULA K. LE GUIN
ILLUSTRATED BY PATRICK WYNNE

ATHENEUM   1992   NEW YORK

MAXWELL MACMILLAN CANADA
TORONTO
MAXWELL MACMILLAN INTERNATIONAL
NEW YORK   OXFORD   SINGAPORE   SYDNEY

Atheneum
Macmillan Publishing Company
866 Third Avenue
New York, NY 10022

Maxwell Macmillan Canada, Inc.
1200 Eglinton Avenue East
Suite 200
Don Mills, Ontario M3C 3N1

Macmillan Publishing Company is part of the Maxwell Communication
Group of Companies.

First edition

Printed in the United States of America

10 9 8 7 6 5 4 3 2 1

The text of this book is set in 15/21 Weiss.
The illustrations are rendered in pen and ink.

Book design by Patrice Fodero

Library of Congress Cataloging-in-Publication Data

Le Guin, Ursula K., 1929–
Fish soup / by Ursula Le Guin; illustrated by Patrick Wynne. — 1st ed.
p.   cm.
Summary: When the Thinking Man of Moha and the Writing Woman of
Maho talk about having a child, two children appear, shaped by the
friends' expectations of what a child should be.
ISBN 0-689-31733-6
[1. Allegories. 2. Expectations (Psychology)—Fiction. 3. Sex
role—Fiction.] I. Wynne, Patrick, ill. II. Title.
PZ7.L5215Fj   1992
[Fic]—dc20   91-29740

FOR SHAWN
FROM UNCLE PAT

There was a man called the Thinking Man of Moha, and there was a woman called the Writing Woman of Maho, and they were friends. Every few days the man would get tired of thinking and say to himself, "I'll go visit her." He would cross the bridge over the river and take the road across the hills, and come at last to her messy house, where the mice flew through the air and the cats collected furballs as big as pillows in every corner. The man would knock on the door, and the woman would stop her writing and call, "Come

in!" She would look to see what was in the soup
kettle, hoping it was soup. Sometimes it was
mice. If it was mice, she would say, "Shoo!" till
they flew out. If it was soup, she would put it on
to heat. While it heated, she would push the

books off a corner of the table, and then the two friends would sit and eat soup and talk, waving their spoons at passing mice. And at last the man would go home to Moha, for he had to feed the cow.

After a day or two, the woman would get tired of writing books and sewing the pages together and binding them into beautifully colored covers. She would stop her work and take the road through the woods and across the hills to visit the Thinking Man of Moha. His house was neat and clean, no cats, no mice, only an old cow in the garden, and she was a clean old cow. The woman would find the man at his desk or in his garden, thinking. They would go into his tidy kitchen and she would watch him mash the potatoes and butter the green peas and fry the fish just so, and then they would sit together at the shining table and eat and talk, waving their forks at flying ideas. And at last the woman would go home to Maho, for she had to feed the cats.

One day as they sat at his shining table
eating the caramel pudding he had made, the
Thinking Man said, "I've been thinking."

"Yes," the woman said.

"I've been thinking," he said, "that it would
be nice if we had a child."

"Whatever for?" the woman asked.

The man thought for some time and then said, "It could run back and forth between our houses and carry messages for us when we're busy."

"When I have something to say to you," said the woman, "I'll come say it myself."

But the man had got the thought into his head and could not get it out. "A child," he said, "could finish the caramel pudding."

"So can I," said the woman, and she did so.

The man paid no attention. His mind was fixed on the flutter of a child's dress as she ran, and the twinkle of her feet.

"Thank you for the lovely dinner," said the woman. She did not offer to help him wash the dishes, knowing that he did not like the way she did it and preferred to wash them himself. She saw that he was thinking, and so she said good-bye and left.

But as she walked through the woods that lay along the hilly road between Moha and Maho, it seemed to her that she saw the flutter of a little red dress before her on the road, and in the dust the light prints of a child's shoes.

When she got home to Maho the mice were all chittering and squeaking in the rafters, and the cats went stalking about with shining eyes. "She's here," they said, "she's here, she's here!"

The woman looked, and there on her bed (which she had not made) sat a little red dress, and there on the floor (which she had not swept) were two little shoes and socks. As she looked, the shoes danced about, and the dress fluttered, and the old broom in the corner jumped up and swept furballs about the floor.

"Where's the rest of you?" the woman asked.

The shoes stopped dancing, the red dress drooped, and the broom fell down. From near the doorway came the sound of a little sigh.

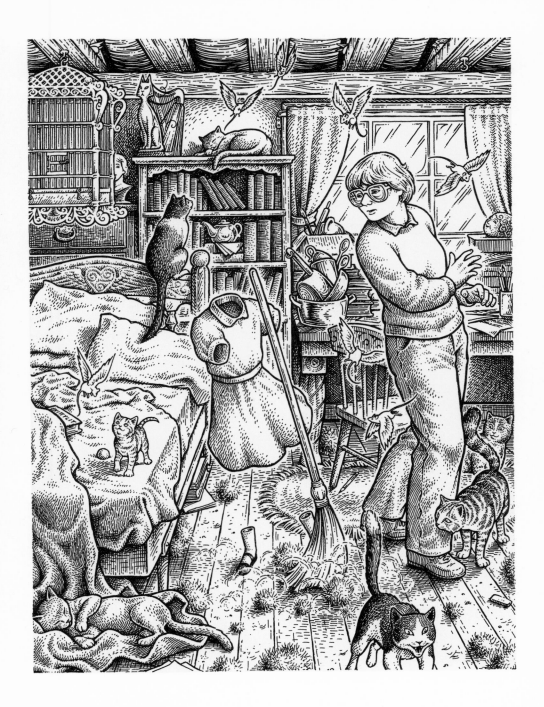

"That man," said the woman, "I think he thinks too much!" She fed the cats. She put what was left from that morning's breakfast soup into the only clean bowl and set it on one corner of the table. Then she pushed last night's dishes away from another corner of the table and got to working at her books. When she looked up, the soup was gone, and so were the red dress and the shoes. The broom lay on the floor, the cats were all asleep among the furballs, and the mice were swooping wildly about the room.

In a day or two her friend came over the hills from Moha for a visit. They had a bowl of soup and talked, and the woman said, "The kind of child that might be useful is a boy."

"Whatever for?" asked the man.

"He could go fishing for us," said the woman. "We never have enough fish soup."

"I'll fish for us myself," said the man, "thank you!"

But the woman's mind was fixed on fish soup. She said nothing, and waved her spoon slowly at a passing mouse. The man did not offer to help her wash the dishes, knowing that she only washed them when all the bowls and spoons were dirty. Soon he started home. Along the way he passed the pool in the river under the willow trees where he liked best to fish. Someone was sitting on the riverbank, a small, quiet person with an angling rod for the trout and a butterfly net for the flying fish. But the man paid no attention and went on to Moha, thinking about something else.

The next time the woman came over the hills to visit, he said to her, "I was fishing, early this morning down at the bridge, and that boy was there again!"

"What boy is that?"

"The boy that fishes."

"Did he catch any fish?"

"Three more than I did," said the man.

"I was writing this morning," the woman said, "and that girl kept sweeping up the dust, till the cats all hid and the mice sneezed."

"I won't have him catching my fish," the man said.

"I won't have her fussing about my house," the woman said.

"I've thought of something," said the man. "Let's trade. You take him, and I'll take her."

"Just as easy as that?" said the woman.

"Why not?" said the man.

All the woman could say was, "I have a feeling it may not be so easy."

As she went along home, nobody walked the road with her. But when she came into her messy house, the cats were stalking about with shining eyes. "He's here," they said, "he's here, he's here!"

From the rafters hung a great birdcage, which was one of the things the woman meant to throw out someday. All the mice were inside the birdcage, eating barley and murmuring happily, and the door of the cage was closed.

The woman considered this for a while and said, "Well! If you want them for pets, you'll have to feed them every day and clean the cage out once a week. Is that understood?"

Nobody answered, but somebody giggled in the pantry.

In the neat and tidy house at Moha, the man finished washing the dishes and wiping the counters and folding the dishcloths. He went into the other room and stopped in dismay. The rug was bunched up into folds like a mountain range. The pillows lay about on the floor like islands in the sea. A castle built of kindling wood

stood on the hearth, and a little expedition of chess pieces was just setting out from the castle towards the rug. As he stood staring at this untidy scene, he heard a soft, small voice telling a story of how the brave people crossed the sea to go exploring in the wild mountains.

"Well!" said the man after a while. "I
suppose it's all right. But when you're done
playing, you must put everything back just so. Is
that understood?"

He did not wait for an answer but hurried
out into the garden to think. Thinking did not
help much, so he fed the cow.

"What do *you* think?" he asked her.

"Moo," the cow said.

The next morning when the woman woke
up in her messy house at Maho, there was a room
in the house that had not been there before, and
a boy came out of it.

"Good morning!" said the woman.

"Good morning!" said the boy. "There isn't
any soup for breakfast, is there?"

The woman looked in the pot and shook her
head.

"All right," the boy said, "I'll go fishing."

"You do that," said she, "and I'll work on a book."

So while he was out fishing, she bound a book in blue and yellow paper. Then when he came home he washed some dishes and cleared off a corner of the table and set it, while she cooked the soup. And they had a delicious breakfast of fish soup.

But as he ate the soup, he began to grow, and he grew to a quite enormous size, so that he could reach up to the birdcage and feed the mice without even standing on a chair. And the house seemed to be quite full of him, so that the woman felt there was hardly room for her.

The boy squeezed himself into his own little new bedroom, but his big feet stuck out of the door, and while the woman tried to work she saw

them out of the corner of her eye. At last she said in exasperation, "Can't you go do something useful?"

"I'll go catch some fish for lunch," the boy said, and he squeezed his way out of his room, with difficulty, for he had been growing again.

Just then the Thinking Man of Moha knocked on the door and opened it and stood there looking thoughtful and uneasy.

Behind him stood a little red dress and a pair of shoes and socks.

"What's wrong with this child?" he said. "Why isn't there more of her?" He looked at the boy. "There's certainly enough of *him*!"

The woman looked at what there was of the girl and at all there was of the boy, and she thought (for she could think, and the man could write, too). And at last she said, "Perhaps it depends on what we expect of them."

"What did you expect of the boy?" the man asked.

"Too much," said the woman.

"Oh, that's all right," the boy said, but he shrank about two feet and began to smile.

"He doesn't have to catch *all* the fish," the woman said, and the boy became his own size, which was just the right size to give a hug to.

"I don't think I expected too much of the girl," said the man.

"No, indeed," said the woman. "Did you expect anything of her at all but a twinkling and a flutter?"

The man said nothing for a while, and then he said, "I did think she could carry messages."

"That's true," said the woman.

They looked and saw two little legs dancing in the shoes and socks.

"I did think," said the man, "that she could finish the pudding."

"I think so, too," said the woman.

They looked and saw the little girl's face, watching them.

"Hey," said the boy, "can she fish?"

"I think so," said the man.

"I think so," said the woman.

But the girl said, "I don't like fishing. What I like is climbing trees!"

And there she was, all arms and legs. She ran out into the woman's wild and messy garden and climbed the apple tree right to the top. They came out and looked up at her, and she tossed an apple down to each of them.

"I think they'll do," said the Writing Woman to the Thinking Man, and he said, "So do I!"

"I think they'll do," said the Fishing Boy to the Climbing Girl, and she said, "So do I!"

So they all lived at Maho and Moha, in and out and back and forth across the hills. The woman's house got a little neater, and the man's

house got a lot messier. The boy made a Trained Mouse Circus, which the cats took a great interest in; and the girl climbed every tree in the woods between Moha and Maho. And they all learned how to cook excellent fish soup.